COMING SOON!

Public Library

COMING SOON!

City Park

for Nathan
—A.Z. & D.C.

Smashy Town
Text copyright © 2020 by Andrea Zimmerman and David J. Clemesha
Illustrations copyright © 2020 by Dan Yaccarino
All rights reserved. Manufactured in China.
No part of this book may be used or reproduced in any manner
whatsoever without written permission except in the case of brief
quotations embodied in critical articles and reviews. For information
address HarperCollins Children's Books, a division of HarperCollins
Publishers, 195 Broadway, New York, NY 10007.

www.harpercollinschildrens.com

ISBN 978-0-06-291037-0

The artist used brush and India ink on vellum and Photoshop
to create the digital illustrations for this book.
Typography by Marisa Rother

20 21 22 23 24 SCP 10 9 8 7 6 5 4 3 2 1
❖
First Edition

SMASHY TOWN

by Andrea Zimmerman and David Clemesha
illustrated by Dan Yaccarino

HARPER
An Imprint of HarperCollinsPublishers

Mr. Gilly is a demolition man.

In the morning, Mr. Gilly puts on his hard hat and heads to work.

He says, "My crane may move at just a crawl, but watch out for my wrecking ball!"

Today some old buildings must come down so a new building can go up. Mr. Gilly starts his motor.
RUMBLE, RUMBLE, RUMBLE.

The crane crawls.
Mr. Gilly pulls the levers.
He turns the crane.

GO!

Swing the ball, hit the wall!

SMASH, SMASH, SMASH!

Swing the ball, hit the wall!

CRASH, CRASH, CRASH!

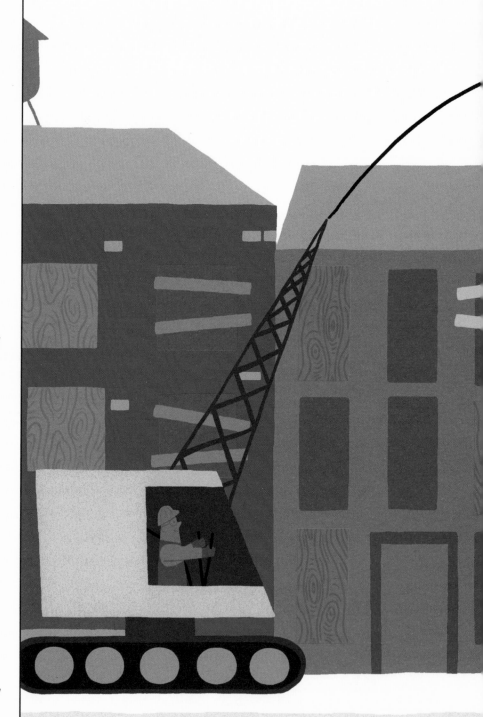

CRUMBLE, TUMBLE, down goes brick.

Is the demolition done? NO!

GO!

Swing the ball, hit the wall!

SMASH, SMASH, SMASH!

Swing the ball, hit the wall!

CRASH, CRASH, CRASH!

CRUMBLE, TUMBLE, down goes wood.

Is the demolition done? **NO!**

GO!

Swing the
ball, hit the
wall!

SMASH,
SMASH,
SMASH!

Swing the
ball, hit the
wall!

CRASH,
CRASH,
CRASH!

CRUMBLE, TUMBLE, down goes glass.

Is the demolition done?

NO!

GO!

Swing the
ball, hit the
wall!

**SMASH,
SMASH,
SMASH!**

Swing the
ball, hit the
wall!

**CRASH,
CRASH,
CRASH!**

CRUMBLE, TUMBLE, down goes stone.

Is the demolition done?

Not quite yet. . . .

It's time to
clean up the
mess!

Brick and
wood and
glass and
stone are
everywhere.

Mr. Gilly
gets into his
bulldozer.

He pushes
the rubble
and rubbish
away.

Is the land all
cleaned up?

YES! The demolition is done.

Mr. Gilly says, "I took those worn-out buildings down and cleaned them up right to the ground."

Now the new building can go up!

And Mr. Gilly heads home.

Mr. Gilly eats his dinner.

Now there's only one more thing
left to do. . . .

Time for bed, Mr. Gilly!

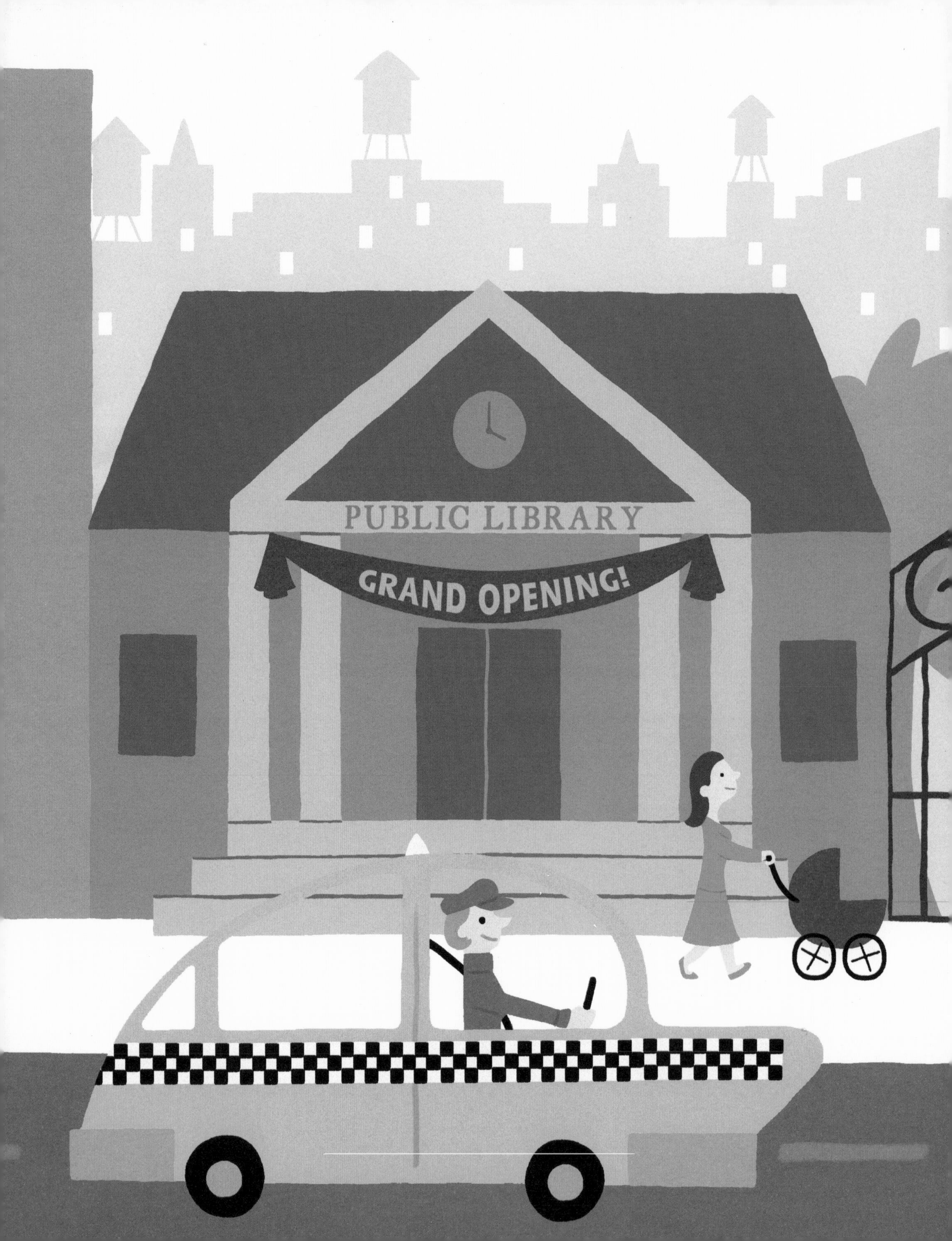
PUBLIC LIBRARY
GRAND OPENING!